Dinner Time

HOLLY HOWITT

Cinnamon Press
Independent Innovative International

Published by Cinnamon Press
Meirion House
Glan yr afon
Tanygrisiau
Blaenau Ffestiniog
Gwynedd LL41 3SU
www.cinnamonpress.com

ISBN 978-1-905614-53-0

British Library Cataloguing in Publication Data. A CIP record for this book can be obtained from the British Library

Designed and typeset in Palatino by Cinnamon Press
Cover design by Mike Fortune-Wood from original artwork, 'Knife and Fork' by Yuri Arcurs, supplied by Dreamstime.com
Printed and bound in Great Britain by Biddles Ltd, King's Lynn, Norfolk

'Harvest', 'Cars' and 'Water' first appeared in *The Final Theory and Other Stories* (Leaf, 2006)
The final line of the foreword 'A great reckoning in a little room' is from *As You Like It*, William Shakespeare, Act III, scene iii, l.11.

Acknowledgements:

Firstly, I must say that this collection would not have been possible without the support, help and advice offered consistently and fairly by Richard Gwyn, whose own collection of prose poetry has long been inspirational. He provoked my interest in microfiction as an emerging writer, and doubtless has been a great influence since – not that I could ever live up to his own breathtaking standard!

Secondly, more than thanks to Jan Fortune-Wood for her enthusiasm and kind words throughout this project. I am so proud to have worked with Cinnamon, and feel that Cinnamon sets a standard for how publishing should be – confident and exciting. Also, thanks to Clare Potter for her advice during this project. Without her I may not have found Cinnamon. And thanks to friends and family who have been thoughtful and sweet throughout.

Finally, my thanks to you for taking a chance on this book, and for having reached this page. I hope you have found some part of this collection to think on. There is no point writing unless your work reaches at least someone, and I hope that this work has found its way to somewhere within you.

Biography:

Holly Howitt was born in Wales, and has lived in and about it all her life, though this is more by accident than by design. She writes fiction in various forms, and is particularly interested in truncated and overlooked genres, such as microfiction and the novella. She has contributed to anthologies and collections both in print and online, and her novels should be out shortly. She currently lives in Cardiff and takes inspiration from her noisy neighbours and late nights. See www.hollyhowitt.com.

Contents

Foreword

I suppose microfiction is its own prescription, a self-explanatory title in a compound word. Little untruths. Tiny lies. Stories that aren't long enough for a short story, not formatted enough to be poetry. Perhaps you've heard of them, perhaps you haven't. In either case, by opening this book I suspect you've decided to take a guess at definition. Haven't you?

I'm not going to tell you what microfiction is and what it isn't. I suppose if I really knew, I wouldn't write it. I know it's short (micro) and that it's a style of literature (and I use the term loosely), but other than that, it's a bit of a fraud – having its own name does not make it its own person, as it were. Perhaps it's suffering from a fragmented identity crisis. Nestling somewhere toothed between poetry and longer short fiction, its genre becomes jagged. It has hallmarks, leaving traces of what it might be, but otherwise it masks its tracks pretty well.

Microfiction famously, and often like poetry, comes together in the final line. For that reason, I occasionally rebel against this formula; My Cat, for instance, or Water, tell you of a greater story looming from the very beginning. It is also usually rich in imagery, again, like poetry, and sometimes seeks to confuse with solecisms or purposefully mixed metaphors. But unlike some poetry, it often contains dialogue, or the fictional gold-standard of having a beginning, a middle, and an end. Saying that, sometimes the narrative starts in the middle – for example, New York. Can you see how easy it is to get yourself into knots?

Some say there's always a twist in microfictions, a stab in the back that dislocates the reader and shows her that, actually, the story has been somewhere else all along (see Harvest). This can be like poetry, but equally relates to the short story. It can feel like a trick, an anecdote, or a sleight of hand. Or sometimes you can learn something, view something differently, like a parable or a fable.

Perhaps the whole point of the genre is its very length. Easy to consume on the bus, tube or in the bath, before bed or with a coffee, there's something satisfying and also unnerving about absorbing a whole world in a few sentences. Perhaps like poetry, again, the story will live on, later, when you least expect it – one word may change the whole story around before you realise. Or perhaps it will end there, with that last sentence – you've seen enough in that one microcosm. Reflecting life, I suppose – the dramas in small bursts; the empty times in-between. A great reckoning in a little room.

Holly Howitt, May 2007

for my parents

Dinner Time

Shoots

On the top of a hill, a blackbird drops a conker at my feet and flies away. The conker rolls once, twice, three times, then stops.

I press the conker to my ear as the wind wraps around me. A small voice inside the conker whispers.

'Tell me the truth,' it says. 'Have you really understood why you're here? Why you're writing this?'

I throw down the conker and crush it underfoot. The wind goads me as I run down the hill. Little do I know that the conker I have pressed into the earth has already started to germinate.

Opening a Box

Silence makes the box pulse under my tight fingertips.
The taut tape around each flap has smeared the skin of the
cardboard brown. I should use a Stanley knife to score the
beating box open, but I won't. Instead, I put my ear to the
sign that reads 'This Way Up' and listen. There is a pulse
inside the box, clean. Someone has left a bloody
fingerprint under the stamp. The Queen's face is
indifferent.

I wonder why I'm not frightened. The beat inside the box
quickens. I unpeel the tape in shaking steps. I open the
box and slide my hand under the heart, each ventricle
spurting at my touch. My shirt is red. As though I have
the authority, I put the heart between my teeth and
devour it all. I close the box.

It was the only way to stop you.

Stone

You are telling me about your new girlfriend, called Lidl or something of the like. It has become my new obsession to call people the names of shops. It gives the person a meaning to me; that their own person itself could never have.

Let me demonstrate. I know a woman who I have been friends with for years, maybe more. I have always called her Woolworth's, because she reminds me of pick'N'mix. She never has an opinion and is always smiling. When her mother died, she sat me down and grinned as she told me.

I know an older man who I once had an affair with, and I call him Sainsbury behind his back because he thinks he's a Lord, but actually is only the purveyor of broken eggs and expensive salami.

And this Lidl is the same. She is cheap and bright and bores me to death, but sometimes she'll say something that'll catch my eye. It was Lidl who once said that Sainsbury was a man who hid his world under his hair. It was only later I realised he wore a toupee. So she was right about that.

And she told me that Woolworth walked as though her clothes were not her own, and she was right about that too. She had stolen all her mother's clothes after she died, and wore them to death too.

But the worst thing she told me has yet to come true. She told me that you were flesh and blood too, that you are just like any other person. But I've been picking at you for years, trying to sculpt you with my ill-fitting chisel, knowing that all I need is a landslide.

I know you are made of stone.

Museum

There is nothing in front of me but people. A tide of children with brown hair, cresting the path of a woman with grey hair, harassed, disinterested, jumper a size too large and threads too warm for August.

She catches my eye and waves a map furiously under my fringe.

'The museum, the museum,' she says, her voice broken, the children laughing. She is unaware and ploughs on, a trail of chuckling, foaming heads behind her.

'On the left, yes? The left?' How do you say 'underpass' in Spanish, I wonder? I flap my arms uselessly and nod, smile, wondering if this is the time that will change everything, the time that I have expected since I stopped expecting anything.

'The white building there. Over there.' I point, feeling my arms wilt under the pressure of it all.

'Oh, thank you, thank you,' she says, no gratitude in her voice, just sorrow. Rain spells out the meaning.

'Thank you, thank you,' chirrup the multitude of children, smirking and moving as one around me. I am submerged by little feet, the smell of sugar. I feel drained, or rather, as if I'm in the process of being drained.

'Okay,' I say, thinking that the only other Spanish word I know is Coca Cola.

'Okay! Okay! Okay!' shriek the children, excitement like green grass, too clean. I feel like a grasshopper, overwhelmed by the height of it.

I smile and laugh, but everything is different.

New York

And when I was there we had to use a lift, you know, an elevator. Because there were so many stairs, everything so tall. So then. We were in the l-elevator, all two of us, and there was a skinny woman in a russet hairy suit at the back. She had smeared red lipstick – I could see it crawling into the fray of skin on her furred top lip. And we smiled, and she looked away, sour, and we all looked forward hoping that someone else would come in because the elevator was crackling and our skins were crisp. But no one came and the elevator was cold and feary. But we smiled at each other anyway because the russet lady simply ignored us and looked at the carpet on the walls. And you took my hand, didn't you? So I took a breath and put my hand in my hair and said, 'Eleventh floor.' Because that was where we were going and she was standing by the buttons. And she stared and her eyes were like big brown mushrooms and getting bigger, and her lips pursed like a horrible rotting fig.

'I do not work the elevator.'

She shut her mouth and her chin pushed forward. And just for a second, you know maybe less, maybe a millisecond, I swear she was a fox on hind legs.

Fears

It's always been the same, I try to explain. Periods and spiders, they're the thoughts I'm bored of. If it's not a furry-legged tarantula, a bird-eating monster, I'm thinking of the heat that makes my insides moan, the dance of my stomach and the heaviness in my knees, then the weightlessness afterwards, like a money spider dancing over my wrists. These are the thoughts that keep me awake, I say. The ones I can't exorcise, the ones that line my dreams and scuttle through my words, wombs and black widows, webs and ballpoint-marked windows.

Is it just me, I ask. Why am I so afraid?

Because you are ridiculous, the woman says, and scurries away on eight legs. My body cramps, expectantly.

The Beach

Wearing my bikini, I am aware of your eyes on everyone else's hot skin. The topless girls' nipples shiver as a warm wind blows sand across the line of loungers; eyes are wiped, but yours are open. Sweat is running onto my lip, and it stings.

I know I can't compete with the breasts, the thighs, the faces.

As I try to listen to your small talk, I have to resort to lip-reading like I always do because my ears are bad and I won't admit it. Later, a man watches me from behind as I wade into the sea. You laugh. I wish I had rocks in my pockets.

Cars

In the garage, where my dad rebuilds and spray-paints written-off cars so we will have enough money to heat the house when the grey comes, my dad sits me on the plate of the car jack and pumps me up so high I can see my own adulthood, where I can pay my bills without waiting for responses from AutoMart and nobody even drives cars anymore.

Harvest

The church, Mary Magdalene, stands opposite our thatched school, and it makes me nervous when I look through the single-paned classroom window sill cluttered with the cress we are growing in see-through boxes. I know the hymns and the right words, but somehow I never understand what the vicar says on his weekly visits to our school hall.

We have a harvest festival but all my mother can afford to let me take is a single, dented tin of red kidney beans, and when I put it on the altar the girls who have brought in their mothers' freshly baked cakes and the boys who have bought in sheaves of their dads' rhubarb laugh at me and point.

And I smile and take a little bow because my dad's the vicar so I know that God will forgive me.

Self-Awareness in the Cinema

And suddenly you realise that the man sitting next to you is – must be – wearing the same aftershave as that man you slept with years ago, and yes, those children sitting in front of you, who smell of chips and fish fingers, those children who are now crying at the scary bit – those children have made you feel protective, and not pissed off like you'd expected, and now you realise that you don't know what's happening – who's that character? What's that person saying? What does it mean? – So you watch the dust streaming through the projector's beam and realise that it's stupid anyway, that this plot and these characters mean nothing to you – and you start to dream instead of your gas bill, your damp, your oven that only cooks on the left side.

Gulls

Tripping along the cracked tarmac, I wonder why there are seagulls in Cardiff. Is it because of the Bay? The slight sea breeze and salty winds that stick to your skin and whip your hair until tenderised into thick, powdery tendrils. Their hard cries make me focus on the mundane, the violence of the gulls' rows; the news, my news, has not yet hit me. The gull perched on the chimney-top has its head to the sky and the cry is too much; it sounds a tear in the clouds or a hole in the sea, forlorn, God-made, irrevocable. Disaster hangs in the air after its call.

A seagull tore me from bed at five a.m. days ago; I sweated with rage till safely in the nest of sleep minutes later. And now, in the hush, as the gull closes her beak and roosts, I feel her sadness as a memory coiled in my ear; the tiredness and the anger and the inevitability of the phone call I just received, as tangible as the soft bird herself.

If he has hurt my sister, I will go there and kill him myself.

Halo

Sitting in the cathedral, there is the vellum of the *Magna Carta* stretched tight behind us, tiny incisive words scratched through the thick yellow skin and catching the quibbles of yesteryear in it, sprawling flies in amber.

I light a votive candle in the private chapel and donate ten pence into a red plastic bucket; the noise turns the tourists around.

An old woman tells her granddaughter that Saint Cecilia is the patron of music, pointing to stained glass as she speaks. I have no way of telling whether or not this is true; only my ignorance can advise me. I do not look at the old woman. But when my back is turned, I hear her say to me, in a cracked and hushed voice,

'You are looking for something that isn't here, you know. The church isn't for you.'

When I leave the exhibition room and pass my candle, the wick is already barren, and smoking. I wonder who heard her.

The Hairdresser

She is very jolly. I only once think to question whether this is an alcohol-fuelled affability. She snips slowly, catching an ear, an eyelid, my neck. I crick to keep away, the scissors snap shut.

I have had three cups of black extra-strong coffee and my breath is the devil's, my heart a deer's. I am as jittery as paper held by a stone to the top of a wall. My eyes pop, my wrists whip at an imaginary assassin. Her fingers bulge and grasp and burn my scalp, nailbeds like open coffins. I shudder; coffee slops. I have lost something in here. I open my bag, look up the sleeves of my jumper, root around in the corners of my eyes, where sheared hair shuffles my contact lenses. Where is it? What is it?

My hairdresser laughs, plunges her scissors deep in my back and pulls out a jellied pickled-onion.

Strategies

Nick sees me before I see him. I can only now pretend to be pleased to see him, and smile, but I know that the few seconds he has on me, catching my sad face, will mean that he has won. He takes my hand, says nothing, and walks me back home from the tired and dirty station where even the pigeons forget to coo.

The next morning, I ask Nick what he would do if one day, I woke up, saw him on the pillow next to mine, and asked who he was. He says he wouldn't care, but as I take his hand I can feel his palm sweating. I smile, my larynx flutters.

Later, I try to work on my novel, but I cannot write anything with him looking over my shoulder. I feel that, somehow, he'll affect my words.

I can never win for long.

Lump

It started with a lump. The lump was small to begin with, small and itchy. Like a pin prick where the pin had been accidentally left in and the skin had started to heal around it.

Nick said that it was nothing, but I knew he was wrong.

The lump began to grow, stealthily in the night, when I couldn't see it, couldn't hear the cells breeding in their mucky little crook under my shoulder blade. Very carefully it felt its way through my back like ivy in brick, picking out the best area to get light and water, just where my t-shirt would end and it would still be showered and soaped.

Tiny little dots started to appear around it, and even Nick blanched when he saw it again. It seemed to leave an orbit where it grew. It looked like a puckered orange was living under my shoulder, and it began to get harder to move my arm.

The lump was on my left side, and Nick said that it wouldn't matter, because I am right-handed. But I always knew that if it weren't for Mrs Williams or my mother's profound 'left-handed people are always odd', I wouldn't have been.

Sometimes my left hand would dart for a pen, try to unscrew a jar, and once it even threw a javelin before anyone noticed what it had done.

So I knew that Nick would never understand about the lump. He began to belittle it, calling it stupid names like 'pea-brain' and 'scabby scallop'. But I had fallen in love with my lump, and I couldn't bear to hear his taunts.

I don't know why I loved it, because soon I couldn't use my left side at all. It was almost as if this little bundle of bits and bobs had given me a stroke. My left hand hung dully from my fattening wrist, where all the blood and fluid collected. I couldn't even raise my arm and the water around it became so painful I wondered if Nick might put it in a sling and nurse me, the way I would expect him to. But he ignored it, looking away when I was in view, picking his toenails, anything.

I decided that the lump needed rest, and as I couldn't use any part of my left side at all now, I became voluntarily bed-ridden. I enjoyed lying on damp pillows all day in our back bedroom, watching the curtains bleach the room red in the morning sun and smelling the mildew grow behind the wardrobe. In the afternoons Nick would sometimes come into my room and talk to me, but as the lump started to swell around my ribcage, the visits grew fewer. His face was tight and pale, and soon it moved to anger, reddening whenever I shifted in the sheets to accommodate the lump, or when I plumped it onto my pillows.

On the last night, Nick came to my room with a scalpel and some brandy.

'Drink this,' he said, offering the bottle.

'No,' I said, refusing to play the game even for one moment.

'Holly, that lump has taken you over. It's making you an invalid and, frankly, you make me sick.'

I rolled away, keeping my lump well away from his murderous hand.

'Holly, I'm going to do it anyway.' His eyes had a look that I'd only ever seen years before, when he had embarked on his worst crimes. He licked his lips thoughtfully, and smiled. He became a tiger, and I became afraid, embracing my lump with my hand and arm. My left side simply lay useless. Treason, I thought.

'You shouldn't even be talking to me, Nick. Who are you to tell me what to do?'

I thought that the unsaid would make him disappear; perhaps even evaporate if I were lucky. He didn't. He remained sitting on the bed, still in his t-shirt, still breathing shallowly, still holding the scalpel.

'It doesn't matter who came first, oh author,' he said. 'I'm here now.'

'You should obey me...' I faltered.

Nick took the scalpel and held it towards my face.

'I'll make you pay for what you made me do. Sitting here, nursing your lump as if nothing had ever happened. Why do you think you've even got a lump?'

I closed my eyes to the burning thought.

Nick lifted the scalpel to my shoulder.

Nick

Nick sits on the step and giggles girlishly. We have found some old photos and he is now fingering one of himself, ten years ago, leaving greasy thumbprints on each end. In the photo, Nick is wearing a red t-shirt that I don't recognise, and a hat that is too small, perched on his gelled scalp like a real pork pie. The photo means nothing to me; I wasn't there then, and I didn't really know Nick. But still he waves it under my gaze and snickers at a joke I don't understand. In the photo, his expression is dead but his mouth smiles, though it looks as if it's concealing a cry. His waist is small and encircled by a male hand, and there is a half-drained beer bottle in his right hand. His left, just in shot, holds the dog of a spliff, glowing in death. No one else is quite in focus or quite in the frame, but there is something in the picture that shows bodies crushed between sweat and heat, and a frenzy that seems to be taking place somewhere else that no one can really see.

I ask Nick what was going on that day, in that place.
'I don't remember,' he says, then looks down at the picture and laughs again.
I ask him if he was at a party.
'I don't know,' he says, bringing the photo closer.

Later that night, after the thrusts and the moans and the sudden calm, Nick sleeps and starts to talk. At first, the words are indescribable, just babbles of some distant language we have all learned to forget. Then I realise that slowly, the words are beginning to make sense. There are tears in his eyes and he clutches my arm, nails digging in, all the time telling me the story. It was that night, that party, that other boy. It is a story I have already heard, a story I have already told, and yet, feeling Nick still warm inside me, feeling his fingers ripping outside me, I am starting to believe that it cannot be true.

The next day, I forget to ask Nick all I need to know.

An Explanation

I barely knew Nick, then. He was distant to me, a tiny speck like the bean of an embryo or the weight of a caterpillar. His words were wrong, so I turned them, smooth and cool. His clothes were wrong; I dressed him in clothes he would grow out of in a year. His family loathed him; I sweetened them with twists and turns that left Nick looking innocent. Whenever Nick needed help, you see, I was there, keeping him company, feeding him and listening to him and guiding him into a life he may not have chosen.

But of course, with any dictator, there are rebels. Those scared of the regime; those who channel underground to change it. Perhaps I had been too arrogant, perhaps too careless. In either case, I was unprepared for what happened next. Nick began to do things for himself. I cannot put it another way. He existed somewhere outside of me: Nick lived, he breathed, was warm. I felt him next to me in my bed, heard him laugh behind me, sensed his touch when the doors were locked. His whistle in the bathroom, his fork in the sink, his breath on my neck. I felt for his hand when I was frightened, but it was never there. He was no longer distant, but he was no longer safe. I couldn't trust his words anymore; felt uncertain of his future. So I wrote him away: sent him to whence he came. I pressed him between sheets of A4, lasered him into the printer, trapped him in documents sucking the energy out of my laptop. It was my very own final solution.

But I was never very forward-thinking; never was the sort of girl who could relate one event to another, leaving empty cartons in the fridge showing a futility in consequence. I may have written Nick away – Nick, my own character, born from my paper and ink, and not my flesh and blood – but I forgot too late that I had fallen in love with him, and can never let him go. It was he I told first when I found the lump on my shoulder, he who soothed me when my neuroses ate into my sleep, leaving me screaming into the night. It was he who suffered my anger when I was hungry, or tired, and he who I looked for when I woke up, feeling the ache of the night before and the heaviness of silence.

Nick knows this, you see; he knows it well, and dances into my dreams when I least expect it, shows himself to me in magazines, leaves notes on my laptop, eats the food in my fridge and prints muddy marks at my front door. I may have written him away, but he will always come back, goading the author in me.

Someone once told me that writing is like giving birth: if so, Nick will always be my prodigal, if papier mâché, son.

Water

There was that time – do you remember it? – where the government said that we must share baths because the sea was evaporating, so we did, you and I, and you soaped my toes and I flannelled your back (most of the loofahs were dead by then) and we thought we were making a difference. Then we were told to drink our bath water as water was precious, and we did. You used that tall glass and I used the blue whisky one. It seemed somehow tastier then, like it looked on those adverts, in that blue glass. Finally we were told that we must only use water if it were to boil one or the other for supper, water being scarce. So I put you in that big pot that we used to put coal in when it still existed and I boiled you dry. After I'd ladled you out of the water, I washed my hair in your stock.

Flesh and Blood

She smiles at the note he left for her, in the centre of the sticky kitchen table. Don't be late. I'll phone you. The note is written in his hard, cursive text; there are no kisses. She fondles her scarf in the hall mirror. It is blue, like her eyes – a present. There is no one else to admire her reflection, cut neatly into the spotted glass, as if always meant to be framed by it. She poufs her hair and smudges her lipstick with a trembling, bent finger. There is a mark on her neck she has hidden with a fold of fabric. It's too adolescent, she thinks. It's my secret. She has forgotten to tell him where she's going – he has, unusually, forgotten to ask. She pouts at her own reflection – her last chance at owning this face, at this time, and feels the heavy thaw of cool panic, snaking inside like a dead man's tongue, still feeling a final spasm of fear. The stars are bright tonight. Shutting the door behind her, she sends him a message, detailing where she will be and until what time, sending it from the phone he bought her. Crossing her arms as she exits the street, she bites back a small amount of excitement, feels it on the necks of the frozen grass.

Daddy

There was a smell to him like parsnips rooted out of red earth and a taste like damp. He sat every night in his chair, hard-backed. He was like a new book, an unbroken spine bolt on the wooden settle. Parched brown skin, crackly against my milky arm. He was Mr Potato and I was Cauliflower, his little fat floret of innocence and gibberish. I was still silent then, not a word having ever escaped my lips since I wailed in the womb. But I would yodel and whistle; loud sounds from his little floury vegetable.

Daddy had tubers coming out of his ears, long feelers like meaty octopus arms squeezing me too tight. Daddy's breath was of the bloody soil, iron and excretion and worms turning against sunrise. Daddy kissed me and waited for me every evening in his hard settle, his feet carelessly tapping the tiles. Soon I was too big to yodel. I wanted my first word to be 'daddy'.

'Daddy,' I said to his back against the settle. Daddy did not move. My voice was a red sky in the morning.

'Daddy,' I said, the insistence coiling in my windpipe.

He was rooted to his chair, repugnant radicles lashing him in. His face was white with beanshooting roots. His many black eyes were watering.

I set a pan of water on the stove.

Grandma

She is eighteen, an atheist, clichéd. She knew it would happen; she just didn't know why it had. She isn't one for a pigeon-hole, a box, a single sentence description. Not for her, the normal life of carrier bags, grating cheese and turning radishes into rosettes. She wears watercolour paints as eyeliner, teal blue, grass green, silken silver. She sews her own dresses, too tight, made out of linen tablecloths, and poses for illicit boyfriends' cameras – pouting, presented, plump.

She dreams at night in her convent cot, but her dreams make her think only of Death. She calls him sometimes, when it's too much. But he ignores her, hearing only the wind begging in his ears, the sea whimpering in his hands.

The thing inside has spun a web so intricate the snowflakes melt with shame. She feels like she is watching an eagle peck at carrion, fascinating and terrifying, and there is no escape. She begs, but only her mattress cares, her pillows cold and damp.

She wakes, fearing something she cannot name. Sweat tickles her eyebrows and the mattress creaks, pacifying. She scribbles a single word on a piece of newspaper by her bed. The sound of the pencil makes her blush. But her dreams are safe now. You cannot fear what you can name; the nuns told her that.

When she wakes she reads the paper. There is that single word, a treacherous name that even Rumpelstiltskin could not have guessed.

Tarantula.

Age

(When my grandmother died, the shock of seeing her coffin is what made me cry. Not because it made the whole situation real, but because the coffin was laughably small. She was always a tall woman: tall and bony. But the coffin was like a teenager's. I wonder what she would have thought of that. She must have shrunk, somehow, when death stopped her heart. So I've vowed not to shrink. I want a big coffin, for people to remember how tall and proud I was.)

I wonder if I'll look old when I die.

Invisible

It is busy in the coffee shop. Elevenses, early lunch or a caffeine transfusion. The coffee shop is called 'Fuelled'. She says she finds this deeply offensive. It implies that there is something essential about tannin, brownies. That there is importance in mocha and coffee grounds.

The large lady sitting behind her is obviously seeking solace in cake. Her cheeks are flushed with the first thrill of butter-cream. She is alone, lips greased with satisfaction and sadness. Her belly gleams.

I look to my companion, who is rosy and round and full of hatred.

'You're so thin it makes me sick,' she says to me.

'You'll waste away,' she says. 'Your hair looks like hay.'

'Maybe I'll become invisible,' I say.

The music is far too flamboyant; the beat burns the soles of my feet. I look at eggs Benedict and know I can never eat. This chair is ruining my train of thought and her voice is like a splinter. I hate the heat in here. I dream of winter. I think of floating through buildings, pulling children's hair. Making a department store bedroom my lair.

'Maybe you will,' she says. 'And goodness knows that's why we all bother. Why we all wait. What we all want.'

I smile, nod, and start to unzip myself from back to front.

My companion and the large lady fight for the skin suit, tea plates clashing, porcelain chipping.

Inside I am air. And I go to search with my unseen eyes what needs to be seen. To be what I have not been. And to go nowhere...

Secretary

She had worked in an office since she could wear high heels and every day had been a potato, filling her time but not doing anything else but making her stomach heavy with pebbles. Her chair was slightly frayed and every time she sat down it smelt like dead people. The coffee machine downstairs was always broken and there was a leak in her window which made her hair fluff.

But she didn't mind her job, because she was scared of everything and at least here she only had to fear the black bark of her boss, and he often had laryngitis. She didn't like Tipp-ex either because it hurt her eyes, but she never made mistakes anyway.

There was one thing she loved about the job, and that was photocopying, because carrying warm bundles of words to her room made her feel like she was in the middle of a sandcastle, or like she was rolling in baked beans. She liked the soft sound of the buttons on the photocopier, so different to her noisy typewriter that snapped like a clam and squirted grey ink. She liked its gentle hum, the way it wasn't in a hurry and sang the same melody like a mother.

Best of all she liked the big flap that was so light in her right hand, swinging down to lick the paper's ears. So she often did all the photocopying, even if it wasn't her turn.

One day she had a stack of reports to copy, one for every office in the country she thought. And that made her smile a little as she clipped down the corridor, even though the smile cracked her bottom lip. She pressed the paper against her rain-damped shirt and it felt friendly. She lifted the papers like ladies' silken handkerchiefs for the kiss of the copier. But as she swooped down, she saw something under the soft glass. There was a woman curled up inside, wearing a tweed suit and smiling and tapping on the other side.

'Come in,' the woman said, and although she didn't hear it she knew what she meant.

She never did the photocopying after that.

Potatoes

It was only when she was in the car park that she realised she had forgotten the potatoes. Everything else was tight in plastic bags, and yet she had missed the potato aisle. But she started the car and, to hoots of annoyance, drove away from the supermarket.

By the time she was home, she had a plan. She mashed together flour and water, peeled it away from her hands and baked it in balls. When the oven told her they were ready, she took them, still warm, and painted each one a stale beige. She even used a dark brown eyeliner on some, pushed bean sprouts into others.

When the guests came, no one mentioned that she had forgotten the potatoes. But as they were putting on their coats, she opened the kitchen cupboard and screamed, 'But I forgot the potatoes! And they were here all along!'

Bitch

After the puppies, the bitch couldn't right herself and severed whatever animal arteries she could sense, until I learnt to climb the apple tree, under whose boughs she would beg me to come down so she could eat another finger, but I never would.

Eye Lid

I dream with my eyes open, because it makes it harder. I see the dusty ceiling light, fringed with spiders' webs like eyelashes, the shelf above my head which holds books I have never read, and I cannot forget the story a friend told me of the girlfriend who wouldn't give him blow jobs because that's what her dad made her do. It is hard to dream with your eyes open; harder still to relent to the horrors of vampires, talking toasters and unicorns that may await you.

List

You were writing a list.
What do we need?
You said.
I wrote on the list.
You re-read, frowned.
You crossed out.
I think you were afraid of putting kisses in the trolley.

Lilies I

The obscene lilies follow me even
As I walk towards the coffin
I want to prise open the lid
Take hold of her wrist
But her box is too small
For my living, fat hands.
In the pulpit
There are ashes in my mouth
Words fall like church mice
The lord is my shepherd
But I want.

Lilies II

The obscene lilies follow me as I walk towards the nave. Their long, yellow stamens only serve to disrupt my walk, my legs like a puppets', string slack.

I want to run to the coffin, prise open the lid, take her face in my hands, shake her eyes open, see the lashed lids slowly awake, a question in the blue. Her box is too small; she was bigger alive. It is only the size of a small child, a laundry basket. A bin.

In the pulpit, there are ashes in my mouth. Words fall like church mice. They scurry away and hide by the font, unused for today.

'The lord is my shepherd,' I mouth. 'But I want.'

Moving Pictures

I don't know who I'm related to here, but it must be someone because this intimate slideshow would be embarrassing for any onlooker less than familial. There are stills of the new, conjugal hotel bed, of the new bride in her bikini, of the new husband with sunburn. There are comments about the size of the suite, the flattering swimwear, the corn-yellow sand. Then the final slide – the two honeymooners straddling the shore, embarrassed of their smiles and nearly blocking the sunset – a classic, where an aunt mouths 'Ooooh' but can't actually let the sound escape, putting a gnarled, ringed hand to her breast.

But perhaps I am the only one to notice, in the background, the dark lithe shape of a man, topless, waist-deep in the red water. I blink, look around the room, but no one has seen the man, instead saying words like 'postcard' and 'paradise'.

I look at the man and, seeming to hold my gaze, he gracefully walks further out to sea, until his head is no longer visible above the still dappled water, and does not emerge.

The aunt drags a hankie over her eyes and says, 'You've captured a lifetime of happiness in that photo.'

I look at my new husband and wonder who has captured that happiness.

Sanctuary

My room is too small for me. I've told her time and time again, but she doesn't listen. It's almost as if she sees through me, these days. I feel like *Alice in Wonderland*, with my feet sticking through the windows and my neck holding up the chimney.

My carpet is still stained brown from the Coke I spilt months ago. She hasn't cleaned it up – she doesn't care anymore, I don't think. And why should I do it? She doesn't even take care of herself now; her face is one huge moon crater and her eyes always seem to be burning. She told Barbara that she might try and get on the dating scene again, and I don't mind, but she won't get anywhere looking like that. But if I told her that, she'd have a go at me for eavesdropping, so I won't.

Not that there'd be a point, because she doesn't listen to me anymore. Perhaps she can't hear – maybe she's gone deaf! She is being very strange in general. Yesterday she came in here (without knocking), ignored me and sat on my bed, crying over that picture of me when I went to Torquay with the school. She put her hand on my pillow and stroked it as though it were alive.

Sickness and Health

I am sick in the mornings, and sometimes I faint. The doctor is nice. It's not hepatitis. It's not an allergy. 'You're not pregnant, you know. Sorry to disappoint.' We laugh; I know. And when he is talking and I see his tired mouth move I think about the boy in my school who paid a girl in my form to put a broken bottle up her cunt.

Alarm Clock

Half-asleep, I listen to my alarm clock smudge the bottom of time, the second hand mired at six. I feel like time is going backwards, lying in bed and feeling no difference between now, the next now, and the now after. Why the hell should I get up? I wrap the scratchy duvet around myself, and count the cracks in the ceiling. Each one tells me a story of another night not sleeping, another murky tale of a muddy night lost by dawn. I keep my head down and ignore my alarm clock, even though it's screaming. My bed creaks in servitude, and I anoint it with a snore. What's there to get up for when everything I want is here?

The curtains sigh, and I for one feel sorry for them.

Capricorn

The goat is exhausted, her ribs opening and closing as if her breath were unravelling only to constrict her body. Her eyes are dry; her white eyelashes flail over the flies and dust she kicked up in the heat, but do no justice to the soft pink flesh. Panting, she lies on her side and, after a beat, lets me rest my head against her flank as I curl on the brown grass beside her. She smells of rotten hay and something else, something almost like hot tyres, something comforting and something like fear. There is the ghost of a bleat, but she is too tired to deny my head its soft, hot place, though her ears flatten, much like a distempered cat's.

I know I should be more careful, be more diligent around her. As my mother said, 'Where does the word capricious come from?' I didn't know, but it sounded bad, made the goat sound bad. 'Capricious,' said my mother. 'She is capricious.' The goat closes her yellow eyes. She has a terrible temper, and fully-grown horns. Her hooves are enough to break a metatarsal, crush a nose – if she wanted. But for now, she is safe. She likes me, likes the way I rake my fingers through her coarse hair and the way I feed her apples that I have picked from the tree, shaking them free of earwigs first. But she can change in a moment, be a devil at will. Last week, she ran her horns through my sister's jumper, disembowelling the soft jersey.

My sister's mouth opened, ready to scream, but nothing came out. My mother was all in a flap – an inch deeper and the goat's horns would have sliced my sister open, she said. I look at the goat, peaceful now in a hazy dream, her coat sticky with sweat. I wish she had disembowelled my sister. But I won't tell anyone that. Because the goat will do it herself, when she's ready.

My Cat

My cat had a miscarriage the day we went on holiday. She prowled around our legs, circling me with childish cries as I packed a jumper because the caravan is always cold. She was damp, almost sweating – although I knew cats couldn't sweat. (I'd done a project on cats months earlier; it had made me runner-up in the Eisteddfod.) Her legs trembled. My parents laughed. She won't stop us, my dad said. Not on our holiday. We giggled – acting so much like a human, it was impossible – she was just a cat, after all.

When we returned, a week later, bickering from being trapped too long in a flatulent box, with only Monopoly as a saving grace, she moaned as we traipsed in, and we followed her to her small cold bed, smeared with blood. My sister said she swore she could see a kitten's body in the liver-like lumps, clumping dry on the nylon, but I think she was lying.

Riding

I am the sort of woman now who has to fill pretty pots with inferior cotton wool buds and soap dispensers with cheaper, Tesco Value hand wash. I use half the washing powder recommended on the back of the packet, and only use my good mascara when I go out. When I was fourteen, a friend came to stay for the weekend, and when my mother opened the fridge door, the girl laughed. Why do you only have Value food, she asked. Your whole fridge is blue and red. My mother didn't hear; the insult was meant for me. She lived in a City; knew what it was to eat Marks and Spencer's cakes at high tea, took trains by herself, lonely in First Class. I couldn't impress her. That was when there were parts of my house you still couldn't go in; pulled back carpets and moisture-heavy doors blocked entry. Even now, I find the smell of damp comforting.

I rode my motorbike around the sprawling fields, careful to fly over hollows left by tired cows. I didn't have a license, and the field was private property, but the girl didn't say anything. She just stood and watched, wearing my mother's old sheepskin coat and my sister's wellies, face white, not even cheering me when I steered the bike whilst standing on the saddle. I asked her if she'd like to sit on the back; I promised to go slowly. She climbed on with panic on her face, a tight smile correcting it. As I took a hill too fast, she clung to my ribs, tearing at me through my puffa jacket, and I couldn't help but laugh.

Satsumas

I eat satsumas from the fridge, when they are cold and firm. I don't like it when I eat two segments together; skin against skin feels wrong. Sometimes, when I swallow a pip, I like to believe that it means something, that I did it on purpose and now some good will come of it. Though it never does.

And this makes me feel that the satsumas have betrayed me. So I bury them, one by one, in the garden, using a bent fork to make hollows for their buckled, pithy peel. Then I stamp down the earth with my bare feet; the earthworms caught in my wake wriggle under my soles. I didn't know I was so angry. When I have finished, I wash my feet in cold water under the hose until they are blue.

I have never felt so clean in all my life.

Wisdom Tooth

The second wisdom tooth came through a month later. It seemed tangled in a jungle of stringy flesh, and was cloven. That, and the pain, made me believe that Beelzebub had taken root in my mouth. Perhaps he had.

I phoned my dentist, who sat me in the squeaky chair that was almost a *chaise longue*, though less sensual. He injected my palate with a bitter twist, and proceeded to wrench the beast out with pliers.

That night, I took my mangled tooth home and placed it under my pillow. All night I couldn't sleep, listening to him talk – words of wisdom, I'm sure, but also words of an insomniac. He muttered about truth and religion and philosophy and, by the morning, my eyes were wide. I pocketed the tooth in a vain attempt to keep him quiet. I had wanted the tooth fairy to come.

World Cup in Wales.

It was the Swedish flag that changed your mind. You didn't think about Ikea, about blond angelic hair on paper-faced boys. You thought about home. 'It's not the same here,' you said, and your face showed me her, your fantasy, sunburnt legs spread wide in the splits, blood-red vulva and fat lobster neck protruding dangerously, the white sheet she lay on already doused with your translucent victory. 'We can't celebrate here,' you said. 'I need to go home. It doesn't mean anything in another country.'

I helped you pack – your white football shirts, your scarlet shorts, your taste for lager that would only last one match. I watched you leave on the train full of yobs, waving goodbye to Wales and hello to England, home of flagged cars, beer-gardens and a belief that when you lost, crying was okay.

I walk back from the station, alone, woozy in the heat, spying the solitary flag that jeered the jingoistic in you. A man in a car calls, 'Afternoon, lûv! Need a lift home?' and I wonder, where is home?

Vignette

A quad bike spurts, puffs, and is braked. A girl – too broad in the beam to be a back passenger really – steps off, skirt too impossibly short for her motion. Her red shoulders are decorated by a line a beads – sweat, perhaps, or worse. Her yellow hair is greased, and she takes some time running her hands through it before retching into a drain. A dog barks.

Her driver – a boy of no more than nineteen and a half – leans forward over the handlebars, and squeezes a spot into his wing mirror. His passenger, finished vomiting, wipes her mouth and pouts.

I watch, silent on my balcony, the crickets covering the rustle of my feet, the gurgle in my throat. I watch as, with his pus-y fingers, the boy scoops her soft flesh to his own prickly chest, gouges out the heart of her with his haunted hands. I watch, and, with some misgiving, wish I were she.

Three Little Words

Creeping down the velvet stairs, my feet tremble on carpet, sucking the noise into their soles. I pad to the kitchen and set the kettle on to quietly boil as you, he, snores upstairs. The snores curl into the steam; sound evaporates in the fog of the dark kitchen. Last night I heard a man calling softly in his garden: Come back, come back. You have to. His pain punctured his old voice, sorrow spilling like the moon's mist. After two hours, I heard him weeping as he closed the back door, but I didn't hear the click of the lock. That's hope, I thought. Or pride.

Pouring the murky water, I douse and throw away a teabag, clasping my hands around the mug, chipped now, but once a favourite. Before all this happened. When I was normal. There are shadows moving on the stairs, voices coming from the bedroom. One voice. No voice. No shadows, either. I shake my head and release my shoulders, tight from the thoughts that chase me awake, the worries and the neuroses and the ridiculousness crawling inside me like a tapeworm, fattened on my fears. I avoid looking into the black mirror, that will taunt me with what no one else can see, and instead I unlatch my door and step into my garden, where I can feel a thousand eyes on me, waiting to strike. I can hear them in the rhododendrons, see the light fall on their irids. I spill a little on the tea onto my hand, but I don't shriek. No eyes, either. I look at my bare feet on the gravel, and wince too late.

All I want from him, the snorer upstairs, the one who doesn't understand, are three little words, three sounds that will change my fears into cool paragraphs, detailed and focused, keep my horrors as abstract poems. Three words that will show I am not alone.

Three little words are all he needs to say. Drinking my tea under starlight, I mouth them to myself.

I believe you.

Dinner Time

I

Every night at eight forty-five precisely, he would say 'Dinner time' and flatten her bones into the sofa, even though the used cutlery lying on the table proved that he had already eaten.

Tonight, she had bathed in garlic as preparation.

'My clove,' he muttered as he bit her collarbone. 'What do you say?'

'Eat me bite me eat me bite me eat me.'

Her monotone tickled as he tasted earwax. He turned her over and bit a hollow of skin at the cusp of her spine, until she cried salty tears, the tip of her tongue tasting yesterday's brine. He crawled away and lay by the fire till he slept with his head in the brown dog's belly.

In the kitchen, she ticked the paper box marked 'Tuesday' sellotaped to the man-sized fridge. She picked at her scabs till they wept pinpricks of blood. Collarbone to knuckle to ankle. She joined the blood with a naked fingertip and knew that just one more day would do it. The dog barked. She folded herself into the dishwasher.

II

There is something about the outside, he thought as he loosened his tongue into her armpit. I do not like the inside, he thought, as he tasted garlic. She has been guarding herself, he thought. He bit slowly into the sore of skin on the knot of bone in her spine and felt her breaths flutter like clumps of reeds caught by the tide.

The sofa smelt of dead skin cells and billowed bad-temperedly as he turned her over. There was a crust of blood on each column. He wrinkled his nose in disgust. His tongue dried, a curly smoked herring, and flapped out of water.

She was silent and heaving over the broken springs that creaked like the moon. He knew he'd given her too much, too soon.

He lay with the dog at the fire and the warmth burnt his back. The dog's belly smelt dank. The man pushed in his nose. Tips of fur tickled. His eyes closed.

III

Today was Ash Wednesday. There were crude remains of charcoal on her forehead from where she had been in the oven.

He was not at home, and the dog was panting by the fire. She could smell its breath in the kitchen, warping the beams to pterodactyl bones.

Each scab rustled under her naked skin, crackling like witches' frying pans. There was a long burn on her arm, the kiss of the oven's uvula.

The door opened and she ticked the box marked 'Wednesday' because she was crispy and mouth-watering. She picked open her burn and smiled at her achievement.

IV

He was late and it made his armpits swoon under too-tight cotton.

No, she was late and it made him retch into his napkin.

The dog was restless, bumping into chair legs under the table and sniffing at the brown-toed feet he found there. The dog knocked the table and a fork flew and landed between his master's toes. He yowled and, perverse, looked down. Spikes of blood grew like tulips in the web of skin and he shouted until she came. He roared. She lay on the sofa and waited, smothering her smile in the cocktail cushion.

He bounded from the table spattering foot blood on the carpet as the dog whimpered and whined; its eyelids closed. He kicked at its belly as his temper rose.

He leapt onto her baring his teeth, chewing on scapula like a goat at bark. He rumpled his face in sudden disgust and distaste.

'Witch, witch!' he screamed as he drew away, his mouth drying with blood and chunks of angel cake flesh. He vomited and the dog swallowed it like soup.

She laughed as she dropped the dog's eyeballs onto the floor.

V

She took the flat paper boxes off the fridge and rolled them into fat pulpy worlds, dampened with the sweat rolling down her spine and bounding over blood. The sellotape stuck to her palm and she peeled it off, staring at the scrape of cells mottling it to eggshell.

'What do you say?' she said and opened the fridge.

His head sat upright inside, eyes waiting for vision in a green glass bowl by his mouth. He was speechless, eyebrows flickering like ambushed eels.

'Eat me eat me,' she said and whistled for the brown dog who was whimpering at the cold fireplace.

'You witch,' she said, and placed the glass bowl in front of its pomegranate lips.

She turned on the oven and started to baste his butchered body in her blood. The brown dog howled and choked on sclera.

'Dinner time,' she said.